The Warden, the Inmate, and 34286

A MODERN-DAY PARABLE
OF A MAN IN PURGATORY

T. Joseph Hardesty

ISBN 979-8-89112-900-9 (Paperback)
ISBN 979-8-89112-901-6 (Digital)

Copyright © 2024 T. Joseph Hardesty
All rights reserved
First Edition

All rights reserved. No part of this publication may be reproduced, distributed, or transmitted in any form or by any means, including photocopying, recording, or other electronic or mechanical methods without the prior written permission of the publisher. For permission requests, solicit the publisher via the address below.

Covenant Books
11661 Hwy 707
Murrells Inlet, SC 29576
www.covenantbooks.com

To the many wonderful men and women of the St. Paul Street Evangelization ministry. May we continue to work joyfully and tirelessly to bring the Gospel message of Jesus Christ to those in need.

Acknowledgments

My heartfelt thanks go to those who lovingly supported my feeble attempt to tell a good story. They include Cindy P., my publishing coordinator at Covenant Books; Beth W. and June W., my proofreaders and grammar coaches; and last but not least, my trusting and forgiving wife, Bev Marie, who makes purgatory bearable for everyone who knows her.

Author's Note

—⋘—

Throughout history, many great writers have used parables to tell a really good story and at the same time encourage the reader to look at one's life from a different point of view. The *Lord of the Rings* trilogy by J. R. R. Tolkien and the children's classic *Chronicles of Narnia* by C. S. Lewis are just two highly recommended works of fantasy (in my opinion, epic parables) of what many can say is happening in our world today. Both engaging epic stories have many characters made "real" by the author and invite the reader to identify with one or more characters. Then there are those eternal parables found in the gospels of the New Testament.

The parables found in gospels of the New Testament are unlike any for several reasons. One is that while the words themselves never change their meaning, the importance to the reader is quite different with every reading. In other words, the personal meaning you receive today from reading the Parable of the Prodigal Son (Luke 15:11–32) will be different when reading it a year from now. Genius! Perhaps this is because gospel parables are much shorter in length than those of contemporary prize-winning authors. Then again, perhaps it's because gospel parables have far fewer characters. Taken together, this suggests to me that the authors of gospel parables are exercising a divine gift for drawing in the reader, encouraging them to walk in the shoes of each character in the parable, and most importantly, inviting the reader to learn something so profound that the reader himself changes his behavior or wishes to change for the better.

The authors of the gospel parables are the best of the best, bar none. Do not take my word for it. I'm not a world-class writer by anyone's measure. Rather, I prefer you take a few minutes and read the Parable of the Faithful Servant and the Evil Servant (Luke 12:34–48). Don't be dismayed if you don't "get it" the first time around or the third time! Gospel parables are so rich that nobody *fully* appreciates their meaning. To help you along, I have endeavored to write a contemporary analogy to this parable. My aim is not so much to entertain but merely to make you wonder. If *The Warden…influences* you to look at your life and your world and to *change* your life and the world for the better, then I will die a very happy man (when that day comes).

So enjoy and be sure to pay it forward.

October 2023

Chapter 1

It's day 8,453. The thin, lumpy mattress makes my back ache like nobody's business every morning, and the crack in the ceiling continues to drip rusty water from the cell above me. Well, I hope it's just rusty water. Ah, hell. I can't complain. I have no *right* to complain considering all the people I've hurt while a "free" man. In truth, I've gotten used to living in this smelly hellhole. I have this eight-by-ten-foot "slice of heaven" all to myself, the stainless crapper flushes when I need it to, and I even have a small window that overlooks the exercise yard. I say to myself, "Not bad, Mikey!" But nobody's listening. I hang my head and mutter those three words over and over, hoping that someday I'll believe things aren't so terrible. Maybe if I share my whole crazy life story, someone out there will hear it. He'll see that something infinitely greater will come along that will carry him through the rough spots. A guy's gotta believe, right?

Officially, I am prisoner number 25421, meaning I was the 25,421st person to be incarcerated in the state penal system. My friends call me Mikey. I began my sentence in May 2000 at Penbrook Correctional Facility. As luck would have it, this state maintains the death penalty. No surprise that Penbrook has an electric chair. Lucky me.

Besides a flushing toilet and a lumpy mattress, I have a lot of time on my hands. I suppose I should be grateful for that. Sometimes, I read the Bible that's in the prison library, but mostly I spend every long-ass day thinking about what my life was like "out there," or what it could have been like…if only.

I admit that I was just plain stupid. I drank a lot, so the things I did weren't just damned dumb; they were hurtful. I hurt so many people in so many ways—and a few people in the worst way possible. The killing of those two young kids! My God! My God! I know in my gut that this cell, this *purgatory*, is where I belong. I've been here a *loooong* time, too! My friend Tommy Boy in the leather shop knows. He's also been here a long-ass time. I *am* a criminal—no two ways about it. I guess I tried to do the right thing on the outside. I honestly did. It's only fair that I get a little credit for trying, isn't it? I never stole from my mother. I didn't kill Eddy in that bar fight with a cue ball even though I wanted to, and I swear on my mother's grave *I did not* kidnap my kids, like they say. What a royal mess that became for me! As God as my witness, I was drinking too much that night, again, and I didn't want to drink and drive to get them home on time. So they stayed with me overnight—so sue me! I thought I was doing the right thing, for Christ's sake! Still, transportation of minors, even if they're mine, across state lines (and in violation of our divorce decree) was a big nail in my coffin. It wasn't the last.

Looking back on it, I can see that the window of my salvation was closing, and it was only a matter of time before I would be locked away for my crimes. Some may find this hard to believe, but going to AA was my last, best hope—even though I hated being court-ordered to go. Every drunk would agree that a pissed-off judge makes for an effective higher power. I was arrested again for DUI and had to agree to ninety meetings in ninety days and time served, or an extended stay in the county's "play pen." Even *my* dumb ass figured going to twelve-step meetings beat the slammer any day. Thankfully, I was able to keep my license and keep my job.

Alcoholics Anonymous meetings were a big, private joke to me…at first. I won't go into detail about the roots of my drinking problem other than to just say I obviously had one—a huge one. After the thirtieth meeting, I began to see things a little differently. Just a little. Being willing to admit that I have a drinking problem, among others, was a big step for me. Did the sun begin to shine out my ass and everyone in my family start singing *Kumbaya*? Hell, no! Even when I made an effort to work the steps, I still wanted a damn drink. Many times, I sat in a meeting and watched all the other white-knucklers paying half-ass attention to an old-timer with tobacco-stained fingers give out one-year sobriety chips. There would be hugs and clapping, which I thought was laughable, and sometimes a sponsor would even bring a cake with a stupid candle on it to celebrate the occasion. It may have seemed silly, but damned if the guy receiving that one-year chip didn't look good. My mom would say he was "born again". I'm not sure exactly what she meant by that, but considering where I am and what I've done, being born again sounds good to me.

The twelve steps of AA aren't easy.

"Really?" I said to my sponsor in the beginning. "You're telling me that I'm going to make a list of every person I have hurt in some way and then go to each one and make amends?"

Leaning in and looking straight at me, he said, "Yep, and, brother, you'll *still* have more work to do after that!"

The way he said this to me—with a warm smile and a fire in his eyes—nearly caused my legs to buckle. Thankfully, my sponsor knew I wasn't ready for making my amends list just yet. To do it right, I had other more important and fundamental steps to take.

After my fortieth or fiftieth meeting, I started to see the light of day. I actually sat down to begin my fourth step moral inventory. My knuckles were not so white anymore, thank God, but damn, this prodigal son has a long row to hoe. With the support of my AA home group and the encouragement of my sponsor, I began the process of peeling back the onion to acknowledge a long list of resentments and fears that I had unknowingly held onto for much of my life. The list included people, institutions, and even principles—like forgiveness, Christianity, and God. This doesn't even include the numbers of people I have harmed in my conduct, mostly sex. I wrote down every instance I could remember, hoping to God that no judge or prosecutor would find out. As I wrapped up my first stab at this crucial step, I came to realize how weak and powerless I was to resist a drink or a good bender to cope with the train wreck my life had become. Another fifteen or twenty meetings helped me feel more empowered to begin the lengthy process of making a list of every person I have harmed and then become willing to make amends to all of them.

Day after day, page after page, I wrote down the exact nature of my wrongs. How humiliating! I could barely bring myself to be honest, but putting it down on paper had a way of making the crap I've done more real. Kind of curious that I actually had been building a prison for myself all along.

After about twenty pages or so of documenting my faults and failings, I began feeling a tug in my soul to take the next step. Then, one night, after one particularly good AA meeting where a fellow "drunk" discussed his eighth step, I talked with Jim about this tugging feeling, and he agreed that what I was feeling was a very good sign, that it was real, and that if my moral inventory was honest and I felt my list was complete, then I could start making my amends in earnest.

"Mike," he said, "listening to you just now, you remind me of a sixteen-year-old kid standing on the edge of a dance floor. The music is grooving and the other kids are out there having fun, but you seem unsure of yourself. You clearly see that pretty girl standing on the other side of the gym with her friends, and you notice that she takes quick little peeks at you when her friends aren't noticing. I understand that you feel unsure of yourself, but you are most certainly aware that you want desperately to get out of your 'comfort zone.' You want to be holding that young lady in your arms and dancing the night away. You seem ready to get in the nitty-gritty of life and live!"

"You're exactly right," I said. "I am tired of standing on the sidelines and watching everyone else in my life just move on down the road, but you and my fellow AA family, you seem to be the only ones who know that I have to clean up my act. Like you said before, one should consult a roadmap before embarking on a long journey."

"Mike, we know you only because you let us know you. You're beginning to understand what you have to do to get and stay sober, but, brother, it's all on you. *You* have to do these steps."

It wasn't easy for me to say "I'm sorry" to people I hurt, but over time, it got easier. Somewhat.

Telling my stepdad I was sorry for whaling away on his car with a crowbar while in a drunken rage was relatively easy. Paying the $1,367 in repairs I owed him was not so easy. Going over to apologize to my next-door neighbor for destroying his mailbox all because he wouldn't "lend" me a few lousy bucks for beer money actually went well. He was quite pleased with the brand-new mailbox I installed for him. And Eddy? The guy I nearly killed in that bar fight? I couldn't make amends with him because he was killed after he mouthed off to a couple of gang members at a biker bar across town. Live and let live, Eddy, you poor schmuck. You should have listened.

One of the more difficult amends I had to make was reaching out to Sandy, a superhot girl I met at my favorite bar back in the day. I remember that I wanted to get her good and drunk so I could have my way with her. It took some time, but eventually, that's exactly what I did. What a shining example of gentlemanly virtue I turned out to be. I didn't even care that her ten-year-old child was sleeping, or maybe trying to sleep, in the next room. I didn't care. God help me, but I just didn't care.

Anyway, I tracked down Sandy's home address, and on my third attempt I was able to muster the courage to knock on her door to make amends. The notion of "thirteenth stepping" her, that is to say, consciously trying to manipulate Sandy, or anyone really, with insincere "sweet talk" for entirely selfish reasons, never entered my mind. Lots of folks in recovery from one addiction or another *say* they just want to help an attractive drunk or a junkie get into recovery, when in truth they may just want to get in their pants. It's terrible, but it happens. Believe me, I understand the temptation of "thirteenth stepping" people, but thank you, God, I had no desire to add insult to Sandy's injury by doing this. I felt terrible for the way I treated her during my drinking days, I said, and I sincerely and humbly apologized. But she was so pissed while hearing me out that she spat in my face and slammed the door. I felt terrible, and not just for myself. All kinds of painful memories and emotions came flooding over me while standing on that rainy doorstep. Surely, it was by the grace of God, *grace* I tell you, that I was able to get my sorry butt to a meeting right then. Christ Jesus, a favorite bar of mine just happened to be down the street! Before you go thinking I might have my drinking problem licked, you should remember that "pride goeth before the fall." I failed to appreciate that wise five-word proverb.

Two years, five months, and fifteen days without a drink. I wasn't white-knuckling my way in life any longer, but I was far from being sober. That's when it happened. I got flat out drunk for no reason at all, and I woke up in some parking lot in the back seat of my car in a pool of my own piss and vomit. Ten minutes later, I tried to kill myself. The judge says I was driving eighty-five in a school zone. Well, yeah, of course I was—I was aiming for a parked cement truck—but God help me, I didn't see those two kids standing next to it. *That* was when I finally hit bottom; *that's* why I'm now serving two consecutive fifteen- to twenty-year sentences for vehicular manslaughter.

"Stick a fork in me, I'm done," I said to myself, handcuffed to a bed in the psych ward of County General. I said this again a year later to my AA sponsor in lockup just before my conviction. I was a dead man walking.

Before I killed those kids, before I threw my life away, I was trying to clean up my life. I attended those AA meetings and always seemed to find one crappy job right after another to pay for rent, gas, and second-hand presents for my kids on their birthdays and Christmas. Speaking of jobs, I worked at a Big-O Tire long enough to get the mother of my kids a brand-new set of tires for her car. I couldn't let her take the kids to school on bald tires. No, in case you were wondering, I didn't steal them. My boss even stayed late one night to let me put the tires on. That boss was a nice guy. He was fair, too, but it was time for me to move on. It might interest you to know that I even went to church, but only when I felt like it.

About going to church—I can't really put my finger on it except to say that I would feel a pull deep down to get my lazy butt off the couch, switch off the Star Trek reruns, and go to Mass at St. Jude, the parish of my youth. How ironic that of all the saints, St. Jude happens to be the patron saint of lost causes. Hey, the shoe fits. Looking back on it, church turned out to be a good place for me then. As a wayward adult, I always sat near the back of church, and nobody bothered me. Actually, it was kind of funny to watch a family stop at the pew I was in, spot me, then nudge the kids to move closer to the front. I didn't stink or anything, but my clothes came from Goodwill, not Macy's, and I often went too long between haircuts.

Being left alone in church meant I could think about what I was doing with my life and focus my thoughts on working the twelve steps. In the dreadful but necessary silence, I would remember again all the damn, stupid, hurtful things I did. *Why, God? Why do I keep doing the things I don't want to do, and can't seem to do what you would have me do*? Now that I'm in prison, I have nothing but time to think about my mountain of regrets and those two innocent kids I cut in half. How, in the name of God, can I make amends to grieving parents filled with loss and hate? Curled up on my thin mattress, it occurred to me that there is absolutely nothing I could do to bring comfort or healing to those parents. Nothing whatsoever. I could throw the switch on the electric chair myself and be willingly fried until my hair catches on fire, and they will still be angry with me. They will still not have the opportunity to watch their daughters play house with their dolls. "What a miserable man I am!" I say to myself.

Mercifully, I am dragged out of the hell of my memories when someone in the prison kitchen starts baking yeast rolls and simmering a big pot of vegetable beef soup. This place is just a stinking pigsty with iron bars. The smell of human sweat mingling with piss ruins a perfectly decent meal every time.

Along the cracked linoleum hallways, I hear the ankle chains of a "fresh fish" being led to cellblock C. I only catch a glimpse of this new guy, but what's to tell? I've seen lots of them over the years. Sometimes they come in groups of ten or fifteen or more; it's a bit odd seeing just one this time. Like all the rest, this poor sap has long stringy hair and an untrimmed beard, but he doesn't look crazy or filled with rage. He doesn't even have any visible tattoos. Keeping my eyes averted is smart here, but I can't help but notice something unusual. It gets eerily quiet as the new guy walks to his cell. Even the guards don't shove or trip him as he walks. They often do that to inmates just for laughs. Oh, what fun we're having here at ole' Penbrook High, I think to myself! Once they reach the end of the hall and turn the corner to C, the familiar routine of jailhouse bedlam resumes. The guards do their bed checks, rattle the doors of each cell, and shut off the lights to the sounds of men arguing or crying and the far-off shouts and screams coming from the nutjobs housed over in cellblock D. Just another night in Hotel Hell.

Chapter 2

Day 8,454 starts out like every other. The six o'clock siren goes off, immediately followed by five minutes of cold water shooting out of the faucet. If you don't wash your face, pits, and privates in that time, well, buddy, you're screwed until the next day—or maybe until your weekly "hot" shower.

Like every morning, there's a nutritious breakfast of cheap cereal with powdered milk, a tiny little apple, and one piece of cold dry toast. Then an escorted walk to the exercise yard.

In no way does the exercise yard resemble a true "yard." A lawn of green grass, tall shade trees, and flower planters would be nice, but no, it's just a sixty-by-eighty-foot cinder block rectangle with fifteen-foot high reinforced concrete walls topped with razor wire, floodlights, and blockhouses manned by guards who probably enjoy deer hunting. Strangely, today they're not carrying their customary assault rifles. Backboards with rusty hoops are mounted on the east and west walls. Many fights break out here because one family or gang claims ownership of a hoop—as if anyone needed a reason to stab someone in here. On the south wall, there's a steel double-door with wire mesh windows in the center. The guards need a magnetic key card and a four-digit code to unlock it. This door is used by the guards to bring prisoners in and out of the yard. A large imposing double iron gate is set in the center of the north wall and leads to the parking lot and administrative annex building. A key card and four-digit code is needed before it swings open, as if by magic.

The weather is good. Saints be praised, nobody is wearing their smelly winter coats or jackets. What surprises the crap out of me is seeing the yard packed with more inmates than I have ever seen before. I overhear a couple of guys say that every inmate in the big house is here. I think every guard and staffer is standing on the catwalks above or looking down from their office balconies. And that's when I see him.

The warden himself steps out onto his office balcony. I assume he's the warden. I never actually met the man or even seen him before. Honestly, I don't *want* to meet him either, and I really don't give a flying fig who he is. The other guys, though, say they've heard rumors about him. He stands up there, all regal, and fecal, and decked out in his three-piece Brooks Brothers suit and red silk tie. It gets real quiet in the yard when he raises his arms to speak. This guy seems different. You can tell right off that he isn't speaking "down" to us. He's speaking to the guards and staffers, too. It's flipping weird to hear and see the top dog speak to everyone as if we're human beings. It certainly holds our attention, that's for damn sure. It's what he says that blows our minds.

"Gentlemen," he says, smiling, "this is a new and exciting day. The governor and the state board of prisons have made an unprecedented change in its philosophy toward the rehabilitation of prison inmates. That fundamental change has come, starting with this very facility, and the man responsible for this change is here with us today." He paused a beat hoping that we would all erupt in spontaneous, enthusiastic applause. Nobody did. He continued, "Many outside these walls would say that the governor's recent decision regarding prisoner reform is unwise and unnecessary. They say that attempting to reform prisoners is reckless and dangerous to society at large. Some want the governor impeached. He has received death threats. Just as many, however, say this new approach to prison and prisoner reform is long overdue. I am in full agreement that this radical opportunity is the only true hope for a better way of life for the incarcerated."

Puzzled and agitated, many of us wonder just what the heck is the warden talking about. True hope for a better way of life? Man, this place is where hope goes to die. Everybody in the yard knows that.

He goes on to say that starting immediately, no guards will be permitted to carry any lethal weapon on their person and that no inmate will be placed in solitary confinement unless it is strictly for his own protection. That starts some heads bobbing. Also, every inmate, even those in cellblock D, will be granted two hours of exercise each day in the yard instead of only one. And hot breakfasts will be offered to inmates starting at seven-thirty tomorrow morning. Lastly, and unbelievably, *three* hot showers lasting no more than ten minutes will be mandatory for every inmate each week. I couldn't believe my ears!

I couldn't believe my eyes, either. Many of us shake our heads in disbelief. A few others mutter curses. More than a few Mexicans and skinheads, who normally hate each other's guts, are actually smiling and shaking hands! What's happening? *And the lion shall lay down with the lamb*, I thought to myself. Is this the apocalypse? Are we all going to be given a steak dinner soon with all the trimmings, then be gassed in our sleep? All these new promises are nothing but a lot of horse crap, I thought. A chronic liar knows a pack of damn lies when he hears them. In a week from now, we will be right back to eating cereal with powdered milk again, and the hapless bastards of cellblock D will have only thirty minutes of daily R&R, if they're lucky.

Back in my cell, I start laughing. It's like attending my first AA meeting all over again. How can so many people be so dumb as to hope for a better life? What a crock! Later that night, the guards make their rounds and hourly bed checks. What was different about lights-out is that I could hear a radio up on tier 4 playing classical music. Nobody yells at the bum to turn it off. Everyone's asleep by eleven.

Chapter 3

Day 8,455 is a day in paradise. The morning wake-up "alarm," if you can call it that, blasts us out of our bunks at seven o'clock. Jesus, the heavenly smell of bacon and hot coffee is in the air! Needless to say, within five seconds after the doors spring open, everyone on my tier lines up and faces in the direction of the cafeteria. A guard, whose stern look makes us walk quickly, has one hand on his baton, ready to do some damage. But we knuckleheads don't care. We're about to have a breakfast buffet fit for a king. But we're no kings; we're anything but that. By the time we arrive at the steam table, the fried bacon is gone. Only things left are warm, spicy hot sausage patties and scrambled eggs made with real honest-to-God eggs.

Standing in line, I remember when I was about ten years old and made my first Holy Communion at St. Jude. I didn't fully understand the theological hocus-pocus Father Hayden, our pastor, talked about, but I believed every word…hook, line and sinker. The nuns taught us the simple explanation that Jesus was the "bread of life," or something like that. It wasn't because I was always hungry, but I vaguely remember as a child, a deeper hunger taking root. I could hardly wait to be one with Jesus, my secret big brother.

Now in line at the steam table, my mouth waters as a line cook reverently slops sausage and eggs on my breakfast tray. The coffee's pretty bad, but at least it's hot and better than the watered-down orange drink we usually get. Nobody complains or fights for extra helpings. It's a flipping miracle. Honestly! After we place our now-empty trays on the cart, we line up and march out for a two-hour visit to the yard.

The air is fresh, the sun is shining, and the basketball hasn't even been punctured yet. The guards toss down a few baseball gloves and some hard balls so some of us can play hotbox or practice throwing a slider. Man, what a great way to start a new day! Something else that few people notice at first is a tall wooden post cemented in the center of the yard that has large eyebolts near the top. I don't remember it being there before, but sometimes you miss things when you live in the same place long enough. About forty minutes into shooting hoops, the warden steps onto the balcony overlooking the yard.

Maybe he was already standing there silently watching us, but soon enough he has everyone's attention. The guards, too, stop pacing the catwalk and turn to face him. Here is a man who, by virtue of his demeanor and title, commands respect. Raising his arm, he drops an even bigger bombshell on us. "Gentlemen, yesterday was a very important day for all of us. It may have come as a shock to some of you to hear about the steps we are taking to improve life here at the prison, and no doubt some of you think these changes are temporary. A cruel joke perhaps. Let me assure you, they are not. In the spirit of transparency, the board of prisons, with the approval of the person responsible for initiating this reform, a man whom you will soon meet, has authorized me to announce that additional rights and privileges will likely be restored to you by Friday evening—three days from today."

Thoughts of sugar plums begin dancing in our heads; it's practically Christmas! Maybe we can get the plasma screen TV returned to the rec room. Perhaps they'll give us free time and the supplies to repair and paint the chapel. Oh, and please, just let me have a box fan for my cell! I'd love to feel air-conditioning, but I'll be happy with a box fan. These and other dreams are interrupted by the warden raising his arm again, saying, "Gentlemen, prior to my arrival here, I have given much thought and consideration to what will soon take place here. The truth of the matter is, each of you is being blessed with the opportunity to go free later today if you so desire."

Nobody says a word. Nobody so much as blinks. The guy next to me begins to sob, so I punch him in the ribs to man up. Meanwhile, I did all I could to keep from laughing out loud. We're all still staring like idiots when the warden turns and gestures for the man of mystery to come out from behind a curtain to join him on the balcony. Lo and behold, it's that new fish I saw two days ago being led to cellblock C.

Like all new inmates, he began his stay in our quaint hotel in C. That's where you go before transitioning to the general population in either cellblock A or B. Any new guys who go bonkers, and some do, eventually get moved to cellblock D with the other headbangers and droolers in the seventh layer of hell. Newbies are given their prison duds and physical and mental exams by a shrink lured here from some Third World armpit. Seldom does the prison shrink speak or understand English, but as long as he can write scripts for Haldol or Thorazine, nobody really cares. Looking up at the new guy standing next to the warden, I don't see him drooling or looking crazy or anything.

The unknown dude stands tall and straight with his hair fixed in a ponytail. The pants of his orange prison outfit are a little big, but he holds them up with hands shackled to a chain around his waist. What a poor substitute for a belt! He's a bean pole of a man, maybe five feet ten, and is either very suntanned for a white guy or light-skinned for a black man. I couldn't tell if he was biracial or from some Middle Eastern country. Asia maybe? Doesn't matter. Prisoner 34286-10 is in Hotel Hell now and stands right beside the prison concierge. As the crowd in the yard waits for someone to say something, the warden reaches into his inner jacket and pulls out a piece of paper.

"Gentlemen," the warden says, "I see that some of you will not, or perhaps cannot, believe what I just said about your opportunity to go free later today. Perhaps this letter signed by the governor and the chairwoman of the state board of prisons will help convince you."

You could hear a pin drop as the warden unfolds the letter. "It reads, and I quote: To Allen B. Cartwright, warden of Penbrook Correctional Facility, June 8, 2023. In accordance with Executive Order 132-45, signed by me on November 15, 2022, you are hereby authorized to implement immediately any and all necessary preconditions, stipulations and requirements set forth by prisoner 34286-

10, who has been remanded to your custody by the state board of prisons, and in accordance to revised penal code, CRS Chapter 7, Section 14, paragraph 3 and signed into law on the 2nd day of October 2022. End quote. Signed, Governor Thomas Ackerman."

Carefully folding and returning the letter to his jacket pocket, he continues, "Gentlemen of Penbrook Correctional, as you can see, I addressed one of the preconditions of the governor's executive order by having that wooden post installed in the center of the exercise yard. In a few moments, you will be escorted back to your cells where you will be given a canvas bag. You will place your personal belongings—clothing, toiletries, mementos, etc.—into said bag, and at 2:00 p.m., you will have the opportunity to be escorted back to the exercise yard along with your personal effects. At approximately 2:30 p.m., prisoner 34286-10 standing before you now will be led out, stripped to the waist, and chained to that post you see before you. Gentlemen, this is a very grave matter. If you have ears to hear, hear me now." Continuing, he says, "A precondition of your early release from this correctional facility requires you to attend and witness prisoner 34286 voluntarily receiving 39 lashes with the leather whip I now hold in my hand."

What the hell! Never in my wildest dreams, and I have had many in my life, could I imagine something so unbelievable, so heinous. Many years ago, when I heard the clank of my prison door closing for the first time, I never thought I'd be set free, much less like this! Looking around at the other guys in the yard, they were probably thinking the same thing.

"In closing, gentlemen, I wish to make perfectly clear to you, and to the guards assigned to your cellblock, that you are not, I repeat *not*, required to pack your belongings or leave your cell. Dinner will be served in the mess hall as usual for those who wish to remain. Lastly, release and full commutation of your sentence from this facility absolutely requires your attendance and active observation of the flogging of this man, inmate 34286. That will be all." The warden and the new prisoner turn and walk away.

Baseballs, gloves, and the basketball lay on the ground, untouched. For the next forty-five minutes, every inmate in the yard is either talking quietly with someone or is absorbed in his own thoughts. A few lean against the wall and cry like a baby. Nobody minds. A few others wander the yard, clenching their fists and angrily repeating the same thing over and over: "Never. No way in hell! I ain't leaving, no way." We finally head back to our cells, just as the guys in cellblock A are being led out to the exercise yard to hear the same bait and switch.

Entering my cell, I notice a green canvas bag with a yellow drawstring on my bunk. All my worldly possessions could easily fit inside it, with plenty of room to spare, but I make no move to touch the damn thing. For the next hour and a half, I just lay there trying to wrap my mind around why a complete stranger would volunteer to be beaten half to death so I could go free. I couldn't figure it out. Maybe this is an elaborate hoax the warden and prison guards are pulling on us. You know, dangling our freedom in front of us just to screw with our heads. I bet the warden and his staff are in his office right now laughing like homicidal clowns hopped up on meth. Could the letter from the governor have been real? It sure sounded legit to me. I don't know. I don't know. I don't know! One thing I do know with certainty is that I don't deserve to breathe the same air as a free man. No way, not after seeing the crime scene photos of those two little girls.

My cell door rumbles open and I see the guys in my tier lining up for lunch. Today is white-bread sandwiches Wednesday. Yummy. Some doofus a few places ahead of me asks a guard if he thinks the bologna and cheese sandwiches or potato salad have been poisoned. The guard says nothing because two of our own guys got to the numbskull first and whack him good. I've heard stories about potato salad going bad in here, so I grab two sandwiches and a carton of milk. Even after sitting down to my "feast," I give my dry sandwiches a sniff test and looked to see if someone tampered with my milk carton. It wasn't. Something about devouring a meal, even a crappy one, while knowing that a man is soon to be whipped within an inch of his life, is all it takes for me to lose my appetite. Ten minutes later, we get up to join the rest of the guys for the walk back to our cells. The pile of sandwiches, I notice, is significantly lower. The potato salad, not so much.

At around one-thirty, I hear and watch a number of my tier mates packing to go. Some had more crap than their canvas bag could hold, so it was kind of funny to watch them hem and haw over what they want to take and what they need to pack. My bag remains empty—I just can't move. Sometime around one-forty-five, I overhear guys pleading with others to hurry the hell up and pack. A few others whisper their goodbyes and good luck. At two o'clock sharp, the doors automatically open, and I stay behind to watch half of the inmates of my cellblock carry their bags down the walkway. A guard leads them into their fool's paradise. In less than a minute, they're all out of sight and the iron doors clang shut, locked tight. It sure is quiet now, enough to hear a toilet flush way over in block A.

Standing on my bunk, I see my cellblock mates through the barred window. They're milling about in the yard, not ten feet away. Few of them notice the idling buses parked near the service gate or the office workers from the nearby administration building placing boxes of files and bundled clothes on portable tables. Just then, the south door to the yard opens, and two guards lead about thirty or so other inmates into the yard. Two more guards secure the door and form the group into an approximation of a straight line. Hey, these guys are from cellblock D! I could tell because some of them wear faded blue coveralls and black rubber-soled slippers given only to folks who live in La-la land. About four or five of the guys, the head-bangers, wear protective helmets, while a few others clench in their mouths rubber bite guards. More than half, I would say, have thick pads of white gauze taped around one wrist or both. God, what a sorry lot.

If I didn't see it with my own eyes, I wouldn't believe it—nor would I expect anyone to believe me! But man, I'm telling you, what a sight. The left side of the service gate opens and the first inmate from D block is directed to the table. There a prison staffer asks the man a question then consults a clipboard. After making a check mark, the employee then directs the inmate down the line to his left. Another staff person finds a manila envelope, hands it to the inmate, and with a smile hands him off to the next staff person, a woman this time. She looks carefully at the man, sizes him up I suppose, then turns to a table behind her and selects a bundle of clothes which she hands over with care. Next and last, the inmate steps to his right, coming face-to-face with the prison warden himself, flanked by two guards.

There is no table separating the warden from the inmate, no menacing security dog or taser-happy guard standing at the ready to shock the inmate into submission. The warden says something to the inmate as the guard on the right removes the guy's waist-bound shackle chain and leather wrist restraint. Holy crap! The man is going free! It's really happening! The same process happens over and over with the other cellblock D inmates. A guard on the left hands each of them a box lunch and a bottle of water then they're escorted to the waiting buses. I could barely make out the bus driver helping them up the steps to get settled in a seat.

Never in a million years will I forget how some of those departing inmates reached out to receive a brief, tender hug from the warden. Others shook hands, while some lowered their heads to their hands, privately sobbing. I'm just glad these poor souls didn't have to see the flogging that was about to happen—as if they weren't suffering enough already. As I watched them boarding their magic carpet ride, I was wondering, what were they thinking and feeling? My God, can you imagine? As the last bus drives away, the warden and his two guards enter the exercise yard. The remaining men of cellblocks A and B greet him with wide-eyed stares and shocked, respectful silence.

The warden crosses the yard and stands patiently next to that eight-foot whipping post, as if he were waiting for a crosswalk indicator to tell him it was safe to continue. He looks at his watch only once, paying no mind to the guys staring at him. Then at precisely two-thirty, the south door opens and prisoner 34286, the new fish, enters the yard. He is preceded by the prison chaplain and flanked by two guards. Trailing behind is Malcolm, one of the most despised and vicious guards employed at Penbrook. In his hands, Malcolm carries a dreadful-looking leather whip. No matter how much my back aches from standing on my bunk, I'm not about to sit down now. Some things are too terrible not to watch.

Prisoner 34286 (I don't even know his name) walks slowly, with tremendous courage, toward the whipping post. The men of blocks A and B step aside for the entourage, shouting, "Praise you, man!" and "God bless you, sir!" But some yell, "Screw the governor" and "Malcolm, you son of a whore, don't do it, don't you dare." Malcolm just smiles. Prisoner 34286's yellow coveralls indicate he was living in block C. But now he's stripped to his waist and secured to the post, just as the warden said. As the chaplain steps closer to read quietly to 34286, the warden raises his hand to speak. Even through the breakproof glass of my window, I can hear him as clearly as if he were standing right next to me.

"Gentlemen of cellblocks A and B! Looking around, I see that some of you do not have your personal possessions with you. No matter. For the time being, it is of minor concern. What matters most is that under no circumstances are you to approach or even try to interfere with the heavy responsibility that officer Malcolm has agreed to perform. Secondly, I will be watching each and every one of you more than I will be watching 34286 as he is being whipped. If any of you so much as turns your back or closes your eyes, you will be returned to your cells. Lastly, Officer Malcolm has been instructed to show no mercy to the prisoner. Should he survive the thirty-nine lashes he is about to receive, the guards, and only these guards standing next to me, will administer first aid and return him to his cell in block C."

Turning to the prisoner tied to the post, the warden retrieves a piece of paper from his jacket pocket and says, "Prisoner number 34286, in lengthy discussions with various members of the clergy and after multiple evaluations of your mental health by board-certified psychiatrists, you formally approached the office of the governor of this state and submitted a petition to take upon yourself the full weight and punishment of the crimes committed by the inmates of Penbrook Correctional Facility. The governor, the state attorney general, the state board of prisons, and select members of the House and Senate Judiciary then held a series of protracted discussions regarding the legal, ethical, and moral implications of your petition. As a result of these deliberations, Executive Order 132-45 was signed by the governor on November 15, 2022, granting your petition."

The warden adds, "So now I ask you, prisoner 34286, do you agree to the preconditions, stipulations, and requirements of the petition you submitted to the Office of the Governor and reviewed by you in your cell last evening? Specifically, that the inmates of Penbrook who wish to be released will be exonerated and be set free in exchange for your accepting the full weight and punishment of the crimes of said inmates?"

Without hesitating, the prisoner responds, "Yes."

Lastly, the warden asks, "Prisoner 34286, are you present here entirely of your own free will? Do you, to the best of your knowledge, believe you are of sound mind and body?"

Again, the prisoner gives a clear, resounding, and convincing "Yes."

The warden folds and returns the statement to his inner jacket pocket, saying in a loud and crystal-clear voice: "34286, you shall now receive 39 lashes upon your back. If you pass out, you will be revived, and the lashes will continue. Let the punishment begin." As the chaplain exits the yard through the service gate, the warden moves next to the cellblock door, saying, "Remember, inmates, my eyes will be on you. If you want your freedom, do not turn away."

Meanwhile, Malcolm approaches 34286, twirling a twelve-foot-long whip behind him. With a smile of hateful delight, the despised guard says, "Don't be afraid to cry or scream like a girl, you pussy." Immediately, several inmates step toward Malcolm, but just as quickly, he turns and gives them such a hateful glare that nobody dares to come closer. Malcolm then positions himself, readjusts his grip on the brass-studded handle, rears back, and reigns living hell on that poor man's back.

The screams are blood-curdling, and the sight of 34286 writhing in unbridled pain and agony is unbearable. I count ten or twelve lashes before I collapse on my bunk and curl into a ball using my pillow to muffle the sounds of hell all around me. Many of the other guys still in my block scream and shout for the whipping to stop.

Others go berserk and pull their hair out or slam their heads against the wall trying, I suppose, to knock themselves out. I just retreat deeper and deeper into my shell, praying for it to end soon. And soon it does. About ten minutes later, the block is quiet and I return to the living. A few of the inmates in the yard soon return to their cells for reasons best left for them to contemplate in the privacy of their heart—or maybe not. Curious, I return to my window to see the inmates of blocks A and B who remained in the yard line up at the service gate like third-graders about to go on a school trip.

Just as before, each inmate who watched the beating had his name checked off the prison roster and is given walking papers and a bundle of new clothes. Each man is given an opportunity to talk quietly with the warden. Many cry as they're led to their assigned bus. Once loaded, they drive off into the sunset. By five o'clock, the guards make their first rounds of the evening in a prison that is currently less than half full. Some might say that what happened hours earlier was a kind of "prison reform", an unmitigated success. Still, I'm not sure what everyone at Penbrook thinks or feels about what they witnessed in the yard earlier. I'm just glad the lashing is over and things can go back to business as usual. You know, three hots and a cot. Speaking of "hots," the enticing smells of fresh-baked bread and beef stew reach my nose before the sound of the 6:00 p.m. dinner gong. Even though I wasn't hungry, I thought I should at least line up with the few guys remaining on my tier. In no time at all, everyone left behind on block A is waiting against the wall at the mess hall door.

Tonight, the guys from block B are fewer in number. They line up on the opposite wall. I have to say it's mighty strange to see every inmate of a major state prison sit down at the same time eating dinner like civilized men. The only thing missing is the white linen tablecloth and silverware. Stranger still is the eerie silence throughout the dining hall. The only sound is that of gross noises of chewing and the scraping of chair legs on the sticky linoleum floor. Nobody wants to look at each other, much less talk. We're all too crushed with guilt for our own crimes, and we just cannot wrap our minds around why another person would willingly take such punishment for us. Was

34286 a fool? Was he nuts, in spite of what the warden said about his sanity? Some of us, like me, are fuming with anger, too. Is it just because we can't understand what just happened? Was it right? Was it fair? Never mind if it was legal! Surely some of us are wondering all this, and more, to ourselves. Pondering in silence is all we can bring ourselves to do. Without prompting drama or fanfare, the remaining prisoners of Penbrook place their trays and plastic drinking glasses in the designated tubs and line up just like good, little schoolboys back at St. Jude. By six-forty-five, we are back in our cells chewing on our thoughts.

Trying as hard as possible, I can't concentrate on the dog-eared Zane Grey paperback I'm reading. The images of that poor sucker getting nearly whipped to death…how can anyone shut that out of their mind? In frustration as much as anger, I throw the book toward the cell bars. It flutters through the air, goes through the vertical bars, and lands face-down on the cement floor, just out of my reach. Ah, crap. Now what am I gonna do?

The question is barely out of my mouth when the warden himself, Allen B. Cartwright, struts down the tier like he owns the joint. He stops outside my cell door, calmly picks up the paperback and hands it back to me without saying a word. But before continuing on his stroll, Cartwright looks me straight in the eye. It seems like we both want to talk; we both want to listen.

"It doesn't take a rocket scientist to see that you're an angry man," he tells me. "Lord knows you have plenty of reason to be. What baffles me, if you don't mind my asking, is why on God's green earth are you still here? You heard the governor's pronouncement. Didn't you believe you could go free?"

What a good question! Taking my sweet time, of which I have plenty, I sit down on my bunk and think about my response. So I speak the truth. "Warden, you have no idea how pissed I am at being lied to all my life. You're damn right I'm angry! But what good would it do to tell you why? I could be sitting on this bunk for the next ten years, and I would still be explaining it all—and for what? Talking doesn't make the rage go away. And since we're 'talking,' how about you tell me the truth about how you lied to us? Earlier you made this grand announcement about how, in exchange for our freedom, we would be required to be in the yard and watch 34286 get whipped half to death. That's what you said, warden, and you lied! Tell me I didn't see the inmates from D block boarding buses and being driven off *before* 34286 was even brought out to that infernal whipping post. Don't lie to me, warden. Tell me the truth!"

Eyeing a Bible I had borrowed from the prison library on the shelf above my bunk, the warden asks that I hand it to him. Since I knew I could get another one from the "do-gooders" who visit Penbrook the first Sunday of the month, I passed it to him through the bars.

Holding my Bible flat in his left hand, he places his right hand on top then asks me to stand so I can look him straight in the eye. "Inmate," he says, "I solemnly swear before you and before almighty God that I will answer your questions fully and truthfully." Feeling somewhat reassured of his intent to be honest, I accept the proffered Bible and return it to my shelf.

"Well, warden," I ask, "what gives?"

"You are absolutely correct," he says. "You did indeed witness prisoners from D board buses and depart Penbrook. When I arrived here a while back, I read the file of every inmate in this prison—including yours, of course. There is no way for you to know this, but of the total population of Penbrook, twenty-three inmates were minors when they committed their offense. Yet those young men were tried and convicted as adults. Ten of those twenty-three had no case file whatsoever in the juvenile court system. I checked. Eighteen of those twenty-three are Black. Of those twenty-three, sixteen are now in the general population with you guys. Seven have severe mental illness, and three others have an IQ of less than 80—all housed on D. And here are more fun facts about D block, since you asked. Of the fifty-seven inmates of D block, twenty-seven have been diagnosed with schizophrenia with paranoid delusion, and eighteen with bipolar disorder. Every one of *those* inmates has attempted suicide at least once since their incarceration. It's anyone's guess when the symptoms of mental illness began. Not even the prison shrink knows, but chances are good that mental disturbance was a mitigating factor in the sentences of these men. Then there are the six other 'headbangers,' as you guys call them. According to their evaluations—one before trial and another after incarceration—these inmates show IQs in the 70 to 80 range. According to the files, one inmate, Jeremy, has an IQ of 78, but thankfully, he is a compliant and good-natured bruiser of 46."

I am as silent as a stone as the warden continues, "Jeremy was seventeen when he stabbed his abusive stepfather fifteen times in the chest while he was sleeping off his latest drinking binge. Turns out Jeremy could barely tie his own shoes and button his shirt. Nevertheless, he enjoyed helping his mother by carrying wet laundry out to the clothesline, washing windows and helping during canning season—simple but very helpful stuff like that. Jeremy had no idea how much his stepfather hated him. The old man particularly enjoyed tripping Jeremy and thought it was hilarious. Jeremy laughed too—you know, go along to get along. Late one night, the old man came home drunk and started knocking the mother around for burning the pot roast and then harder for getting "uppity" with him. Things went from bad to worse, and in his drunken rage, the old man threatened to cut the mom's throat with a butcher knife if she didn't shut up and mind her place. Jeremy witnessed all this while peering from around the corner. Had that old man just put the knife he was holding back into the drawer, I think he'd still be alive today."

The warden relates the rest of the sordid tale: "When the police arrived around eleven-forty that evening, Jeremy was still holding that butcher knife in his blood-soaked hand. It was a slam-dunk case for the local prosecutor, who also happened to be gunning for district attorney. The understaffed and overwhelmed public defender had never had a defendant in a capital murder case before, but he assumed that due to Jeremy's below-average IQ, the jury could not possibly convict him. But they did. Murder in the first degree if you can believe it. During the sentencing phase, several elderly neighbors testified that Jeremy often retrieved their newspapers from their shrubs. Two other neighbors watched as Jeremy regularly helped young children cross the street near his home. Even the chief of police, who attends the same church as Jeremy and his mother, testified that Jeremy ought never to have been convicted of murder. It was all for nothing. Two days later, the jury sided with the prosecution and decided that Jeremy should be put down like a rabid dog."

Up until this morning, Warden Cartwright says Jeremy was happily sitting on the floor in D block, oblivious to his impending execution, and playing with a set of Lincoln Logs that the guards bought him. Boring his eyes into mine, the warden asks, "Since now you know the gist of Jeremy's story, do *you* think Jeremy is a menace to society? For that matter, do you honestly think he deserves to be strapped to a chair and fried by three jolts of electricity until his eyes pop out?"

My silence is enough of an answer for him. After a bit, I ask, "So what happened to Jeremy? Did you send him home?"

"Oh, hell no," the warden says. "Two days after the funeral of the stepfather, Jeremy's mother was beaten to death by the victim's brother. No other family members give a tinker's damn what happens to Jeremy. The prisoner reentry program for convicts found a church group in a neighboring state that has a one-bedroom apartment and a job for him, working part-time with a local Habitat for Humanity. With state-mandated and compassionate supervision, Jeremy should thrive on the outside."

I can tell the warden is about to wrap things up and move along, so I stand up and approach the bars. As if by reflex, not to mention common sense, he steps back, but continues to make penetrating eye contact with me. "Before I leave you to your paperback," he says, "I should add that contrary to what you may be thinking, I did not empty out cellblock D completely. The social workers and psychologists on staff, in consultation with the board of prisons, have advised me that, through no fault of their own, ten inmates of the total population of D are too dangerous to themselves or to others to warrant release back into society. Lastly, there are four other inmates on D who have no family whatsoever, and who are so mentally ill that it would be cruel and inhumane to just abandon them like a feral cat in a city or town. No, those poor souls will probably live out the rest of their lives being cared for by professionals who can now give them the care they deserve."

Cartwright admits to this being long-winded answer, but saying, "You asked for and you deserve the truth, the whole truth and no bull. The short answer I'll give you is that 34286 and I agreed that the men on D should not have to watch that lashing, not in their mental state, and so it was decided that the time they already served in their purgatory was more than enough. Call it a compassionate release if you want. What I don't know is why *you* decided to pass on a perfectly good opportunity to go free today. I'm not going to pry." After a moment's silence, he added, "And, hey, you may be happy to know that the wounds of 34286 have been tended to, and he is able to sleep on his side." The warden tells me to rest. "Tomorrow is a new day, and God isn't done with you yet," he says. With that, Allen B. Cartwright continues down the tier, saying a quiet goodnight to each of the remaining prisoners.

As the last of the lights on the block wink out, not a creature is stirring, not even a rat. The same could not be said out on the yard, however. Just beyond my window, I can hear the quiet talk of guards collecting balls and gloves. That and the sawing down of the whipping post.

Still unable to sleep, I turn on the overhead reading light and flip open my Bible. Luke chapter 22, the description of the Last Supper, jumps off the page and draws me in. After an hour, I fall into a restless sleep, listening to a solitary cricket outside my window singing its mournful yet joyful cry.

Chapter 4

The theme song of *Gilligan's Island* plays in my head as soon as I wake up on day 8,456. If I had to listen to that earworm all day, every day, I know I'd end up over on D block. The smell of hot coffee and sizzling sausage patties finally knocks the tune right out of my head—thank you, God! The guys on my tier line up quickly, but we find that the cafeteria is only half-filled. It's surprising, though, to see inmates from A block scattered among us. *Is this all that's left at Penbrook?* I wonder. Some inmates may have decided to skip breakfast and stay in their cells, but they're in the minority. The aroma of hot food drives everyone to come to the table, even if it's loaded with heart-stopping cholesterol and sodium.

Out in the yard, the sky is overcast, but not a rain cloud is in sight. The air is cool, with a nice light wind blowing from the northeast. Listen to me. I sound like a meteorologist on Channel 8! I notice there is something different; there are no balls, gloves, or basketballs. And that damned whipping post is gone too, thankfully. The dried blood left from yesterday's scourging must have been washed away somehow. For whatever reason, the guards on the catwalk won't toss down any toys for us to play with, even when we ask politely. Two hours of just standing around can get old pretty quick, so I walk the perimeter of the yard, doing a few deep knee bends and keeping my head down. I'm not into calisthenics or any of that yoga crap, like the younger guys. Prisoner 34286, beaten and bruised, is presumably sleeping or maybe having something brought to his cell, so that made me feel good. Who knows? Perhaps this day will be uneventful.

But I'm wrong. Thirty minutes into our two-hour exercise period, the warden—flanked by Malcolm and two other guards—enters through the service gate. Looking past them, I don't see any buses lined up. I was hoping that I'd see one or two waiting to drive more lucky souls off to the promised land.

I have seen many things as a guest at Penbrook estate. Some I'd like to see more often, like the nice lady visitors who come every Thursday afternoon. Some horrible things I can't unsee, like yesterday's beating. Today's image is a new one. A guard trailing the warden carries a three-foot chain attached to a clearly marked sixty-pound dumbbell. At the opposite end of the dumbbell is a metal collar big enough to fit around a man's neck. The authorities walk to where the beating post was, now a stump, and one of the guards unceremoniously drops the dumbbell to the ground. Just like yesterday, everyone just stares silently at the warden in a nonviolent Mexican standoff sort of way. After about five minutes, the cellblock door opens, and 34286 emerges, followed by two additional guards. The dude walks stiffly and slowly, but his head is erect, and he looks cleaned up in a new prison jumpsuit. This is the first time I am able to see him up close. Without making a sound, I edge closer, along with a few other inmates. The warden whispers a few words to 34286, and he whispers back. Satisfied, the warden turns to us and raises his hand to speak.

"Gentlemen of Penbrook! Good morning to you all. I hope you slept well and that you enjoyed your breakfast. You are deserving of both, and I mean that sincerely. Some of you may have heard rumors that cellblock D has been emptied. I am here to assure you that this is not the case. While the majority of the inmates of D have indeed been released, as was my prerogative, a number of inmates remain, and must remain, in that block for the foreseeable future. You will rarely come into contact with these men, but I want to assure you they are being well-cared for. Now onto the matter at hand. It may please you to know that starting next week, $50 will be automatically added each month to the balance of each inmate's commissary account."

That announcement brought a big round of applause and good neighborly backslapping. "The caveat," he continues, "is that you must spend it each month or lose it. Also beginning next week, inmates will be given the opportunity to make two additional outgoing phone calls per week lasting no more than fifteen minutes each, instead of the current one phone call per week. Lastly, inmates will have the opportunity to receive a haircut every six weeks by a volunteer barber instead of every three months. I am happy to say that these and other improvements in the living conditions at Penbrook slightly exceed the national average."

Then Cartwright reminds us that we were given a canvas bag yesterday. He says we'll have an opportunity to use those duffels later today for the same purpose, if we so choose.

"After lunch at approximately 1:00 p.m. today," he says, "the guards of your respective blocks will come by your cell to confirm that you still have said bag and to give you a replacement if you do not. At 2:00 p.m., you will again gather here in the yard where you will be provided with a second opportunity to be set free. Like yesterday, your attendance is purely voluntary. However, should you choose to join us, you must bring your personal belongings with you, and you will be required to actively observe the event. Gentlemen, I hope to see you at two o'clock."

With that, Malcolm leads the warden and 34286, flanked by the four guards, back to the cellblock door, where they disappear.

Two hours later, the men on my tier take hot showers, our first in weeks, along with clean prison-issued underwear and new jumpsuits. Where our inmate number normally would be affixed, there's a fancy Penbrook Correctional logo—pretty cool. Around noon, the smell of soap and deodorant linger on the block then mingle with that of hot coffee and vegetable beef soup. Heavenly! Everyone's in a good mood and feeling human again as we calmly, even politely, walk in single file to the cafeteria to join our brothers from A block for lunch. Waiting for us is a pile of dry bologna and cheese sandwiches, but the coffee is hot and fresh, and the soup is made from scratch, with honest-to-God chunks of carrots and celery! Nobody talks while we eat. To top it all off, individual servings of chocolate cake with white icing are brought to the tables. It's like discovering that Santa is real!

By one o'clock, everyone is back in their cell, each man staring at the ceiling or his navel. Finding neither of great interest, I stand on my bunk to gaze out my window facing the yard. Cigarette butts and a few candy bar wrappers are scattered about, and a solitary crow perches above the guardhouse. I can't see any airplanes in the sky, flying couples to romantic beachfront resorts or happy families headed to Disney's Main Street USA, eager to hold hands with Donald Duck. The most disturbing object in the yard is that sixty-pound dumbbell, the sun glinting off its attached chain and neck collar. I have a bad feeling about this when I sit back down on my bunk and eye the canvas bag.

I could toss a few things in that bag and be ready to go in a matter of minutes. But then I think of those two innocent little girls I killed, the sad and hateful look of their parents when I was sentenced, and the countless people I lied to, manipulated, stole from, and *hurt*. I could never live with that on the outside, not in a million years. I won't begrudge any inmate who accepts the warden's offer for clemency, especially if he has only a few years left to serve. But I deserve to spend the rest of my life in Hotel Hell. It's 1:45 p.m. I hear fellow inmates on the block packing their stuff, cajoling guys in nearby cells to get ready and say their goodbyes. At exactly two o'clock, the prison doors open as if by magic, inviting those who want to leave this dog-and-pony show to line up on the walkway. For the second time, I refuse the tempting offer, preferring to watch my brothers head to the exercise yard. I resume my perch on my bunk.

Sure enough, several ugly Greyhound buses, spuing out diesel fumes, are parked beyond the service gate. The portable folding tables are set up and populated with file boxes, bundled clothes, and boxed lunches. A moment later, the cellblock door leading to the yard opens and the inmates from A and B begin their entry to the antechamber of freedom. Most of the prisoners who smoke light up using the electric lighter a guard plugs into an outlet on the west wall. A prisoner from my block (who has a joke for every occasion) pulls out a paper plane he is famously known for making. He lets it fly. One time, he actually gets one of his planes to fly over the wall, never to be seen again. Another paper plane flies through the open window of a guardhouse. Rumor has it that this guy spent three days in solitary for a rude message he had written in the folds of the plane. Finally, after waiting about five to ten minutes, all heads turn to the service gate as it opens. Here comes the warden, four guards, and prisoner 34286.

The six stand in the center of the yard, surrounding the sixty-pound dumbbell. Again, nobody speaks, and a familiar hush descends over the gathering. A minute passes before the warden steps forward. "Gentlemen," he says, "I am truly glad to see you here today and that you brought your belongings with you. Many of you are undoubtedly glad to see 34286 with us today. None of you saw to completion the lashing he received yesterday, but I assure you that he received that brutal punishment voluntarily. While he has not completely healed from yesterday's ordeal, he has made it clear to me that he wishes to see all of you live free and genuinely happy lives beyond these walls, and to that end, he wishes to proceed with today's punishment as prescribed by him. I sanction the upcoming punishment and will honor his wishes. Before we begin, I request a volunteer to please step forward."

A thirty-something inmate with a shiny bald head and life-affirming tattoos covering both arms walked confidently up to the warden and stood with bulging arms crossed and head cocked slightly. The guy is huge, to say the least. A maroon, purple, and green tattoo of two mermaids with long flowing hair in an erotic embrace covers one arm the diameter of a bowling ball. It is rather fascinating to watch how the tails of the mermaids actually moved when he flexed that arm. They even shimmer if the sunlight is just right. Pretty trippy. The other arm of the inmate standing before the warden is covered with black-and-brown miniature portraits of young women about the size of tennis balls. From where I am standing, I can count three but there may be others. Prison yard gossip has it that each face is of a woman he raped and left for dead.

The warden asks the inmate to first inspect the dumbbell to ensure the chain is firmly fixed and then lift it. The unknown inmate checks the chain, but lifting the dumbbell is more challenging. "Do you have any doubts, sir, that the chain is firmly attached?" the warden asks. The inmate, straining at the weight he is holding, quickly shakes his head no. Satisfied, the warden then asks loudly, "In your opinion, sir, do you believe this object weighs sixty pounds?" The prisoner answers quickly in the affirmative. "You may lower the weight to the ground now. Thank you, inmate."

"Does anyone doubt that this object weighs sixty pounds?" the warden asks those assembled in the yard. No one speaks. "That precondition completed," he says, "then I must inform you that 34286 is hereby required to carry this weight the full eighty-foot length of the exercise yard until he can no longer do so. Furthermore, 34286 has agreed to have the metal collar fitted and secured about his neck. Finally, none of you is permitted to assist him in any way, verbally or physically, nor will you interfere in any way with this punishment. Stay clear. It's best for you and the prisoner that you remain silent. You must, and this is very important, *you must* observe this man's every move. Gentlemen, let me be perfectly clear that this precondition for your release is non-negotiable. I will be watching each of you as you watch 34286. Do not let his punishment go to waste because you decided to pick up cigarette butts." Turning to address the prisoner, the warden says, "Inmate 34286, please kneel and place your hands on the weight." He does so.

Next, the warden asks Malcolm, the guard, to step forward and place the metal collar around the prisoner's neck. He does this with ease and, perhaps, a little pleasure. Lastly, the warden tells 34286 to start walking.

Two minutes stretch into five as 34286 struggles, carrying the heavy burden. After the fourth-round trip, the prisoner stumbles and falls to the ground. He soon stands up, though, and resumes a slow, tortured pace. Returning after reaching the west wall the sixth time, he stumbles and falls again. Thinking he may have passed out, a guard is permitted to approach the prisoner. A well-placed jab with his baton gets 34286 moving again. With legs and arms trembling under the strain, with sweat pouring down his face and stinging his eyes, with blood weeping from wounds received the day before, he carries the weight of our crimes another 120 feet before collapsing for a third time. He's lying unconscious on the ground. Just then, the forgotten crow atop the guardhouse caws loudly and flies off.

This torture lasts fewer than ten minutes, but it drains every bit of strength and perseverance from 34286. Several of the men light up their smokes again, slowly inching quietly toward the service gate. Meanwhile, a guard assigned to remove the electric cigarette lighter directs the warden's attention to three inmates kneeling in the northwest corner. Praying? I don't think so. That same guard then approached the three inmates to find them enthralled in a game of craps. Each guy gets one solid smack with the guard's baton and is hauled to his feet and directed toward the cellblock doors, along with their canvas bags. Another guard approaches 34286 lying prostrate on the ground and removes the neck collar. He checks to see if he's dead. A third guard slowly pours a large cup of water on 34286's face; it has its desired effect, causing 34286 to slowly sit upright in the grit of the yard. He's permitted several minutes to rest before being gently helped to his feet. Slowly and with great care, he's escorted to the cellblock door as the men of A and B blocks offer him words of admiration and gratitude. One man cries shamelessly with his face turned to the sky and his arms raised in praise for his deliverance from hell. Then the warden and two remaining guards walk calmly through the inmates gathering near the service gate. No one rushes the gate or even jostles to be first in line. It's as if they knew they were already living as free men. Knowing what is about to take place at the gate, I sit back on my bunk and begin to cry. I just can't help it. They're happy tears for those men who were set free through the suffering of another, and they're tears of great sadness and remorse for the inmates and me who remain locked in our prison of guilt and shame.

I must have walked a mile, pacing circles in my cell, as I thought about the horrible and wonderful things I have witnessed these past two days. How can the warden have the legal authority to exonerate two-thirds of a prison? How far will he and 34286 go to offer freedom to those of us left behind? Who, for crying out loud, *is* 34286? These and larger questions turn my mind and my soul into pulp until I'm jarred by the dinner horn.

Going through the cafeteria line takes all of two minutes, but it sure makes my stomach rumble. Salisbury steak with real gravy, mashed potatoes, and seasoned green beans, with room left on my tray for a second piece of chocolate cake. The mashed potatoes are made with honest-to-God real potatoes, and the green beans even have pieces of onion and country ham, just like my mom used to make. The cake's a little stale from lunch, but I don't mind. I can hardly wait to grab a seat, any seat, and dig in. Finding a seat is easy. Out of thirty tables, ten are empty. Everyone's there, chowing down, with plenty of elbow room. Even Malcolm and some of his friends sit nearby enjoying the same fare. *That* has never happened in all my time here. The food is hot and looks so good that it lifts the spirits of a few of the inmates.

There is room at one table that has two intelligent-looking guys, and we soon make guarded but friendly eye contact. That's a good clue that they are safe and willing to talk. One inmate, Sammy, licking his fingers, says that this whole thing going on is just one big charade.

"I'm telling you, me and several of the guys on my tier are convinced that this is just a cruel joke that the warden and his cronies are pulling on us. In fact, we have a bet that by 8:00 a.m. tomorrow, every inmate we saw leaving Penbrook would be back in their cells. That or some other schmuck from another overcrowded Ivy League "big house" of correction will be slumming here. Just you wait, this place will be packed as tight as a can of sardines in no time, and the joke will be on us. Not me man, I'm no fool. I've got a carton of cigarettes riding on it."

"Oh shut your piehole, Sammy," Jimbo says.

My other talkative dinner tablemate, Jimbo, finishes a second helping of cake and slowly lowers his fork to his tray. Brushing a few crumbs from his mouth, he says that he thinks most inmates in this facility believe deep down that they're guilty as sin and should never see the light of day. "Me, on the other hand, I'm staying right here as long as I can. Not because I want to—I hate it here, but, brother, I know for a fact that if I were to be released back into the wild, I will burn down another apartment building just because. I can see by your eyes you think I'm as crazy as a sewer rat," he says. "Well, maybe I am. Lord knows how bad I want to get my hands on a pack of matches. Today, though, I know better than to try and guess what's going on in the minds and hearts of other men—especially those inmates who were set free. I don't care if I burn down a building and kill a dozen people in the process, but those guys who left today, I believe something happened to them that can't be seen under a microscope."

We sit in silence staring at our empty dinner trays for a few minutes until Jimbo looks up at me. What I see is not the gaze of a man crazy with desire to set fires, but instead, a fire of wonder. With a single tear running down his cheek, he asks, "Could it be possible that I could be forgiven for what I did? Thankfully, I didn't kill anybody in the fires I started. None that I know of anyway, but God, I'd do anything to not have this burning desire to burn things! I'd love to see a sunset over the mountains just one more time before I die. Is it too late for me?" he asked.

Sammy just scoffs and picks up his tray and walks away. I just sit there in silence with Jimbo as long as we can, wondering the same things.

By seven o'clock, I'm back in my cozy cubicle trying to find my place in the Zane Grey paperback. I hear a fight break out between two inmates on the tier overhead. With the prison population so small now, all the remaining inmates of A block have been moved to B. *What's the damn fuss about?* I wonder. Every inmate has a cell all to himself now, and each cell has a window looking out onto the yard. This is a step up for some of those jokers from A. Finally, things settle down to the point where I hear two inmates sing a beautiful Black spiritual in two-part harmony, and then another inmate at the far end of the block plucks away on his guitar. Just as I'm being lulled to sleep, I hear the familiar sound of the warden's footsteps.

"Well," he says as he approaches my cell, "I see you're still here, inmate, although I've no idea exactly why. The food in this place is getting better, but it's not true home cooking. Not by a long shot. Care to tell me what's on your mind?"

Sitting up, I shrug my shoulders and wonder aloud what life would be like for the men who were released today. We speculate on that one for a few minutes, deciding all we could do was hope they make the best of their new lease on life. They will be put in touch with resources in their community, so again, they should do well. Warden Cartwright adds, "You've surely noticed that all the inmates have been relocated to your block. Even those in C block have been transitioned over. Only 34286 remains over there. What blows me away," he says, "is the effect we're having on prisons all over the state. Suicide attempts have declined across the board, the use of solitary confinement has nearly been eliminated, and incidents of assault have come down across the prison population. Skeptical wardens and even a few state governors are beginning to take notice."

"And that's not all. Somehow, the press has gotten wind of the reforms, and ministers and clergy of every denomination are preaching about this like there's no tomorrow. Even judges are using their discretion to move more non-violent offenders into targeted, cost-saving court diversion programs. Lastly, and it's too early to tell, but I heard from various sources that crime reports everywhere are inching downward, to the great relief of police departments. If this reform keeps up, it's very possible that we will consolidate all remaining prisoners in the state into just one facility. Wouldn't that be wonderful?"

Then he asks me if I need anything, maybe a better pillow or roll of toilet paper? A current newspaper? He even offers to stop by again in the morning. I politely decline all his offers. Pulling out a Rosary from his pocket, he asks if I might like to have it. A prisoner on tier 4 is making them, he says, and giving them away along with instructions on how to pray with it. Without a second thought, I reach through the bars and accept the gift and instruction pamphlet. The warden smiles, says a sincere goodnight, and moves on to make his appointed rounds.

My thoughts, however, turn back to the consolidation of prisons in the state. *Would* that be wonderful? I wondered. Maybe for the state budget, but what kind of men and women would be imprisoned in that facility? I already know the answer to that. That prison would be filled with men and women who are not only hardened criminals, but people whose hearts, minds, and souls are so hardened by doubt, resentment, guilt, rage, and shame that they might not see that a better way of life is available to them for their asking. Utterly forsaken by society, those inmates would probably be living in a crappier place than I am in now—if you can believe it. And just as I think this, I begin to cry. Nobody seems to notice. Just as well, I was so wrapped up in my own spiritual stink that I preferred to be left alone. I was thinking what it would be like to be a leper, then I laughed inwardly at the realization that *I am* a leper! Oh, I don't have a bell hanging around my neck to warn people away from my putrid contagion, and a leper may be free to walk about the earth in a futile search of bread and companionship, but much like the leper, I reek, positively *reek*, of unrepentant guilt and shame. Of course, we are shunned by society! Even when we don't mean to be, we are a menace! So I ask you, God, as much as I ask myself, how can society ever welcome me back when I am so totally convinced that I am unworthy of acceptance? And just like that, my thoughts took another turn.

Wasn't there a story somewhere in the New Testament about a Roman centurion? Yes, I remember, he was a high-ranking military officer who was also admired and respected even by the Jewish elders in the region. He also had a slave. That was not unusual, but what was different about this guy was that he valued his slave very much. Imagine that. The slave was near death, and the centurion asked Jesus, through some Jewish intermediaries, to come at once and heal his slave.

There are several things in particular about this story that fan the flames of hope in me. One is that I remember (as a child) saying similar words to Jesus during Mass that the Roman centurion said to Jesus just outside his home: *Lord, I am not worthy that you should enter under my roof but only say the word and my servant shall be healed.* If this incredible story is to be believed, the centurion asked in a spirit of confidence that his slave be healed. In the spirit of authority, Jesus healed the slave that instant. Boom! I get it! Jesus wants me, a slave to crime, to be healed, but I have to invite Jesus in first. I have to ask. But it can't possibly be that easy, can it? And just like that, my thoughts took yet another turn.

I am not only like that of a "sinful" leper or a dying slave, but, God, I am a prodigal son, to boot! I am just like the son in the New Testament parable of Luke (chapter 15, verses 17–32) that had selfishly forfeited his father's entire inheritance on the drugs, sex and the rock-and-roll of the day, and thus rightfully deserves to live in this pigsty of his own making. That sounds familiar. Whatever made the prodigal son think that after what he had done, he was still worthy of forgiveness and being reunited with his loving family? The parable says that while in the pit of despair, hopelessness, and pig slop, he "came to his senses"—whatever that means. The prodigal son was reduced to begging for scraps being tossed to filthy pigs, and here I am hoarding rancid, baloney sandwiches to eat when the good stuff runs out. What a pair we make! Hunger couldn't possibly be what brought the prodigal son to his senses. It must have been something else. But what? *What* did the prodigal son have that smacked him upside the head?? Slowly, ever so slowly, it began to occur to me that the prodigal son had absolutely nothing whatsoever. As the parable says, he had, in fact, squandered *everything*.

He had no money, no friends, no hope, no direction. He had absolutely nothing. Nevertheless, the prodigal son must have heard in his heart his father's call to please come home. It may have been just a whisper of a voice, but he paid attention to it. The more he listened to that quiet, gentle invitation, the more capable he became of believing that he was worthy of returning home.

Lying on my bunk and feeling tears slowly dry on my face, I kept saying, "I want to come home, I want to come home. Please, God, if it be your will, help me find the way to come home to you."

That evening, I sleep like it was the night before running a marathon.

Chapter 5

Day 8,457 begins with thunderstorms and torrential rain squalls that not only clear the dust from my cell window, but seem to push the litter in the yard toward several six-inch storm drains. It's a Friday, not "Good Friday," mind you, but it sorta feels like that in an odd sorta way. The five-star breakfast buffet is nothing to write home about, but for this place, it rates near the top. Bacon today and scrambled eggs, toast with a choice of jelly, and oatmeal! Cereal with powdered milk is becoming a distant memory, thank God. Because of the continued rain, yard time is postponed.

So on our way back to our cells, one guy who fancies himself a pretty good whistler serenades us with a few bars of the 1969 Burt Bacharach song "Raindrops Keep Falling on My Head." A few inmates boo him good-naturedly, but they're in the minority. The rest of us eggheads give him a walking, clapping ovation. I'm back in my cell for only a few minutes when, with great pleasure, I obediently submit to the required hot shower and shave. In fresh clean prison garb, I sit on my bunk and reach for the Rosary and instructions the warden gave me the night before.

I don't know much about the Rosary. But I do know a few of the prayers. Everyone knows the Our Father, and every Catholic worth his salt knows the Hail Mary. That's 90 percent of the Rosary right there. The other prayers that make up the Rosary are new to me, but they're spot on. I didn't know that certain events in the life and death of Jesus are emphasized on different days of the week when someone prays the Rosary. Also, I read that if you say the Rosary, reflecting on the life of Jesus, you pray to receive the same spiritual gifts and virtues as everyone else in the world who's also saying the Rosary. That's pretty powerful stuff!

Feeling rather self-conscious, I begin with making the sign of the cross and simply say the written prayers in the prescribed order. If you pray the Rosary on Friday, you think about Jesus in the Garden of Gethsemane prior to his arrest (Luke 22:47–52). This is followed by his scourging at a pillar for the sins of all mankind. Next, Jesus is crowned with painful thorns, followed by his carrying a heavy wooden cross. And lastly, his death on the cross for the terrible crimes and unrepentant sins we have committed. As I say the prayers and meditate on these "sorrowful mysteries," I lose track of time. My mind, heart, and soul sit with those terrible events of Christ's passion and death, and soon, I realize how tremendously similar they are to the events that have unfolded before my eyes over the last few days. I am so engrossed in reliving the mysteries of the distant and recent past that I'm unaware that my cell door has opened. A guard yells for me to get my lazy butt out and line up for yard time.

By midmorning, the rain stops. The air is refreshingly cool, and a breeze helps the sun dry out the wet spots in the yard. A number of guys already have started a game of catch, and about a dozen others are forming up to play a rather aggressive game of scratch soccer with a new ball the guards tossed down. Thirty minutes into the second half, a goalie sprains his wrist, making a save, and I volunteer to take his place. Hey, as long as I don't have to run like a deranged chicken, I'm ok with that. We are up by three points when two guards come through the service gate. Two more guards open it fully to allow another guard to drive a midsized utility cart into the yard. Following the cart is the warden, Malcolm, and lastly, a maintenance worker carrying a small toolbox. Well, the soccer game is over now, so we all make way for the cart to travel to the center of the yard. Secured on the back of the cart is one of the most hideous devices ever invented by man: an electric chair.

It takes four guards to lift the beastly thing and position it solidly on the ground where the whipping post had been. Wordlessly, and with seemingly practiced care, another guard uncoils a fifty-foot length of thick electrical power cable resembling a gigantic poisonous snake. This he runs from the chair to an electrical port in the east wall. Next, the maintenance worker bends down, opens his toolbox, and begins connecting what appears to be electrodes and leads running from the right arm and left leg of the chair to a small black box located near the bottom of the right rear leg. Finally, he connects the thick power cable to the black box and then connects a ten-foot cable that ends in a red thumb trigger. He hangs the trigger onto a hook at the back of the chair. It takes all of ten seconds for the inmates of Penbrook to know what is about to happen to some poor soul. It also doesn't take a genius to know that the victim is a guy lying on his bunk in C block. The warden wades into the crowd of shocked inmates, demonstrating his trust and confidence in our knowledge that he is not the enemy. After several moments of collective silence, the warden lifts his head and says, "Gentlemen, your time in the yard is now over. Please return to your cells and contemplate what is about to happen here at approximately four o'clock this afternoon."

As we file through the cellblock door, I happen to glance back over my shoulder in the direction of the service gate. No bus is parked in the lot to take anyone to the promised land.

We're in our cells by eleven. No lunch is served; no showers are allowed; no haircuts are permitted. Anyone with a radio or personal television is told by their neighbors to not even think about it. Absolute silence descends upon the block like a cloud. It's a peaceful cloud, so peaceful that I take down my Bible and grab my Rosary to begin praying: "Dear God in heaven, I don't want 34286 to die. I don't want him to die for what I did. Oh God, I am a sinner. A miserable despicable sinner who has lost his way a long, *long* time ago and in so doing hurt so many people. I am so sorry, God."

With tears streaming down my face, I recall each person by name: Jill, Ruth, Bobby C., Teresa, Alice K., Sandy, a second Sandy, and a third Sandy, and Greg, Linda, Michael P., Jim, and Jimmy S., Patty, Bryan, Jeff, Scott, Tina, Helen, and innumerable nameless people I remember hurting in a variety of ways. The list is endless. I thought I had made complete amends in AA prior to my incarceration, but *this* remembrance went on and on.

I realized that the judge in my trial, acting as my "higher power," did for me what I could not do for myself, namely, lock me up so I couldn't hurt anyone else. "God," I say, "I have no right to call you *Father*. I am utterly lost and have no ability to stop my hurting—I hurt so much. I hurt, Lord God, all the time! I am utterly and completely powerless to save myself, but you, God, only *you* have the power to save—if only I surrender completely to you. Jesus surrendered completely on the cross, and you, God, saved him from death. I know in my heart that I am nothing but a miserable criminal and sinner. God, will you save a wretch like me?"

Without realizing it, I find myself on my knees, fingering the beads of my Rosary and I'm transported to the Garden of Gethsemane. There I watch and hear Jesus telling his heavenly Father how afraid he is to die, that he is afraid for the salvation and well-being of his many followers, and that his death on the cross for the sins of the world will be in vain. Suddenly, the Jesus I see kneeling in the Garden of Gethsemane turns his eyes toward me and his look of love and compassion penetrates my soul. In the blink of an eye, Jesus is now 34286! And oh my God, rather than sitting on a glorious throne of dazzling gold, he is strapped to the electric chair in the exercise yard!

Standing on either side and slightly behind Jesus, I see two young girls who have the face of angels. A golden glow surrounds them, and their robes are pure white. I recognize them immediately. No longer do they have severed limbs, mangled torsos, or post-autopsy stitches. Rather, they're the adorable little girls I killed twenty-three years, three months, and two days ago. They are whole and absolutely radiant with love and joy and happiness. Best of all, they melt my heart as they gaze upon me. Somehow, I remain on my knees, but I am not alone. I become aware that right outside my cell is the warden, also on his knees. His eyes are closed and his right arm is lifted in praise and prayer. In his left hand, he too is holding a Rosary. He doesn't acknowledge me, but he prays silently for my salvation. "Where two or more are gathered in my name," Jesus says to me (me!), prisoner 25421-5.

His loving eyes are so warm, so gentle, so peaceful, and so compelling that I cannot resist his call to follow him. Why on earth would I not? How could I not?

"Jesus," I say, "you are my Lord and my God. *You* are my savior from this life of sin, crime, and misery. There is no other. *You* are my light, my salvation, and my Lord. Jesus, I surrender all that I have and all that I am into your care. Take me, Jesus. Take me as I am, a lowly sinner."

Then I say a prayer that is recited five times throughout the Rosary: "*Oh my Jesus, forgive us our sins and save us from the fires of hell. Lead all souls to heaven, especially those most in need of your mercy.*" When I look up, the warden is nowhere to be seen. It's like he was never there. But I'm positively sure he had been kneeling just beyond my cell. But I sense that I'm not alone, not by a long shot.

The Lord speaks directly to me: "Michael, you are no longer 25421-5. I call you my friend and my brother. I died for you a long time ago so that you might live with me in my kingdom now and forever. Through prayer and worship, I will give you special gifts of the Holy Spirit that you are to use to bring others to me. I want you, and I need you to use these gifts to help build my kingdom on earth as it is in heaven. Michael, my dear brother, I have loved you from the beginning of time itself. I call you by name, brother Michael, to come and follow me."

Now, call me crazy, but I am so overcome and delirious with joy that my flowing tears turn into laughter that lifts my soul to the heavens. "Precious Jesus," I say, "I will gladly crawl through broken glass and follow you to the ends of the earth. I will be a prisoner for you, Jesus Christ, but I also remain a prisoner of this facility. How am I to follow you anywhere?"

Jesus responds: "My beautiful son, there are many rooms in my father's house, true, but whether it's called a room or a prison cell matters little to us. There are today, many thousands of brothers and sisters like you around the world who spend their entire lives in perpetual prayer and adoration of my sacrificial love for the world. They are in prayer every day, all day praying for the conversion and well-being of souls, and they live in cells much like yours. My angels and saints are prepared to assist and intercede for them in their chosen vocation—and for you as well. So, my brother, how you choose to follow me is entirely up to you. All I require is that you pick up your mat and walk with me."

The vision of Jesus and his two heavenly angels soon fades, but I feel an indescribable sense of lightness—the weight of all my guilt and shame is gone! "Lord Jesus," I exclaim, "I am your servant. Show me the path you wish me to take, and I will take it."

With my eyes still closed, I hear the unmistakable sound of the click and rumble of my cell door opening. For the life of me, I don't know how it happens, but I wake up standing in front of the warden on the other side of the service gate. The wall clock behind him reads 3:45 p.m. Standing to the left of the warden is a woman who happily hands me a bundle of new clothes and a boxed lunch. Allen Cartwright himself hands me my document packet and a new Bible, and because I am still in a daze, he escorts me by the arm to a single bus in the lot. His parting words are kind, true, and necessary to hear.

"Mike," he says, "you are being sent like a sheep among wolves, but have no fear. You are more free now than you have ever been in your life. Discipleship, however, will not be easy. Leading others to trust in God is seldom easy. You will need much earthly and spiritual support. Pray! Pray like your life and soul depend on it. And let's not forget, you still have many amends to make. Getting reconnected to a twelve-step recovery group can be a big help. Now go in peace, my brother, to love and serve the Lord."

The bus holds six other former inmates of Penbrook, so finding a seat is easy peasy. The door shuts and we pull away, just as the digital clock above the driver reads 4:02 p.m. The receding sounds of the gates of hell on earth closing and of men screaming in torment are horrible, there but for the grace of God go I, I say to myself. Soon those terrible sounds become the soft Christian rock songs I hear coming from the bus speakers and can begin to breathe again.

Several miles pass along the tree-lined country road before I open the large manila envelope that was given to me at my departure from Penbrook. On a separate sheet of embossed stationery from the office of the governor is the following:

Executive Order: 167-37-2023
Subject: Full pardon of prisoner number 25421-5, inmate of Penbrook Correctional Facility.
Date: 25 June 2023

Know All Men By These Present that inmate 25421-5 of Penbrook Correctional Facility, whose name is Michael Hartledge Thompson, has served in full his sentence for the crime of involuntary manslaughter (criminal file, CR 456-4-1986) and is hereby ordered to be released immediately.

Furthermore, copies of this Executive Order will be on file with the state clerk of the criminal court, the parole branch of the State Board of Prisons and this office no later than 30 days hence and will be made available for inspection upon request.

Signed this 25th day of June in the year of our Lord, 2023

Thomas Ackerman, Governor

A separate piece of paper lists a number of names and addresses of private boarders in my hometown vetted by the prison board who, for a modest fee, provide meals and accept short-term living arrangements. Employers sympathetic to prisoner reintroduction as well as hospitals, medical clinics, and even soup kitchens are also listed. Finally, in a separate document, my medical and dental history are found. Reviewing my medical history, I'm reminded of the time in August 2005 when I was stabbed in the thigh for not moving fast enough to another table in the cafeteria. And then there was my dislocated shoulder in 2008. I was instructed to tell the prison doc that I tripped at the top of the stairs of tier 3. A young officer Malcolm who stood behind the doc just stared at me, daring me to say anything contrary. Well, Lord, if there's anything I've learned, it's to turn the other cheek. I'll add two more people to my prayer list now.

Looking at my new Bible, I try to find the verse about turning the other cheek. Was it in Mark's gospel? I wasn't sure. Flipping to the beginning of Mark, I find a prayer card between two pages. Whaddya know? Back in the day, we kids called them Vatican playing cards. Our parents and grandparents would collect and proudly display them in their bedrooms, just like I did with my baseball cards! I treasured my Pete Rose card more than any other. Now, instead of Rose or Bench or Perez or any other of the Big Red Machine, the Cincinnati Reds, I'm now holding a card depicting my man, St. Jude. On the back is a beautiful prayer that I know he is probably saying right now on my behalf.

I turn to the front of the Bible and find a surprise handwritten inscription: *"For God so loved the world that He gave His only begotten Son, that whosoever believeth in Him should not perish, but have everlasting life" (John 3:16).* It's followed by these words: "I will love you, brother, until the end of time." It's signed, simply, 34286. Beneath the number is what looks like a single drop of dried blood.

And there's another handwritten note inside the front cover. It's written on the stationery of my hometown parish church, St. Jude. It reads:

Dear Michael,

> *You have a long and difficult journey ahead of you, but fear not—you are never alone! The parish family of St. Jude is looking forward to seeing you at Mass this coming Sunday. Mass begins at 10AM. Come early and stay late. You will need spiritual food to sustain you in your new life and, brother,*

you will be amazed by what I can whip up on the altar with just a loaf of bread and a cup of wine!

In Christ,
Father John
Romans 1:11–12

I flip over to Romans and tears begin to well up in my eyes as I read the verse. I know I have to meet this Father John. Attached to his note and invitation is a $50 gift card that has the word *VISA* stamped on it. I have no idea what it means, but I hope it might come in handy someday. Without a wallet, I tuck it into my Bible. I figure it's a safe place.

Chapter 6

―᙮―

Standing on a podium in front of a large gathering of friends and adopted family in the St. Jude Parish social hall, I begin to share my story: "It's day 8,823 of being clean and sober. I would not be alive today had it not been for the love, kindness, and intervention of many people. My name is Mike, and I am an alcoholic."

I wait a beat for anyone who may want to say "Hi, Mike!" And I'm happy to hear a good many give the familiar and appreciated reply. To break the ice, I quickly admit that I'm also a sinner. Then I continue: "Several people I wish to acknowledge in my journey are here tonight. They are sitting among you. I won't ask them to stand because I value their anonymity, but if they want to, they are more than welcome to be recognized. Briefly, there's Tommy Boy and Warden Allen Cartwright of Penbrook Correctional Facility, and my Alcoholics Anonymous sponsor, Rick."

Rick stands up from his seat in the third row and gives a quick wave. "I also want to thank the good Lord for my mother, Monica Thompson, who passed away last year. That woman prayed for my soul and safe-keeping long before I squandered my life away on drinking and pursuing a hellish life. Looking upward, I say, thank you, Momma! Thank you for never giving up on me. I'm glad you were alive to see me knock on your front door when I was released from prison. I love you dearly, and now you can rest easy. Rest in the arms of our Savior. I know you're listening, so please remember to have my favorite summer squash casserole hot and ready when I join you at that great feast in the sky.

"I also want to express my deep love and thanks to Father John, pastor here at St. Jude. He has been a wonderful spiritual mentor to me. Lastly, and this man is at the top of my gratitude list, is someone many people know only as prisoner 34286. I was never told his name, but in the short time we were incarcerated together at Penbrook, I came to believe he was sentenced to death for a great many horrible crimes—not one of which he committed. Prisoner 34286 did for me what I could not do for myself. He saved me.

"On the evening of June 25, 2023, I was sitting on a bus being driven away from Penbrook. As I looked out the window, the trees, the grass, and the pastures never looked so beautiful. They were resplendent with life. The smell of fresh mown hay was intoxicating, but in a *very* good way," I said with a smile and a wink. "While being driven down a country road, I opened the Bible that I had received earlier in the day. I started reading the gospel of Luke, chapter 12. Here's my condensed version of Jesus's explanation of the parable of the faithful and wicked servant. I noticed several folks who brought Bibles were opening and turning to that chapter.

"In verses 42 to 48, Jesus describes four different kinds of servants. First, there are those who turn their lives over to the master of the house. They do this each and every day in the desire to do only his will to the best of their understanding and ability. These are vigilant and faithful servants. Jesus himself says their reward will be great in heaven.

"Second, there are those, hopefully few among us, who turn their backs completely on the will of the master of the house. These are people who want absolutely nothing to do with God's plan of salvation and choose instead to live a life of greed, lust, gluttony, and vice. Surely, you would agree that that these servants, people who live to selfishly take all they can get out of life, will spend eternity in a lonely, tormented hell. Obviously, these are the wicked servants Jesus is referring to in Luke 12:46.

"Then there are servants like us, like all of us, who are neither fully vigilant and faithful or totally wicked and evil. Looking out from where I'm standing, I see a nice mix of faces. Some white and some black, some youthful and others, God bless you, just tired and haggard. I don't have to know. I don't need to know which of you believe Kamala Harris walks on water or that the sun shines out of Donald Trump's rear end. What matters to me right now is knowing in my heart that every person in this room has done something terrible, perhaps many times, and they live with the regret of this memory to this day. If you have sought forgiveness from God and true reconciliation with those you have harmed, then praise God! You can know in your heart that you are helping to build the kingdom of God. However, if what you have done continues to eat at you and destroy you from the inside, ruining not only you but making life more painful to those around you, then please, I beg you, get right with God. Don't wait another day! In fact, Fr. John is here with us now, and I know he will happily make time to see you one-on-one for a good ole' heart-rendering sacrament of reconciliation.

"What concerns me, though, is not so much those who know in their hearts that they have done a grave injustice to another and repented for it, or have yet to do so. No, I'm more concerned about folks like us who have done terrible, even heinous, acts in the past and just don't care all that much. I'm not being judgmental here. God knows I have no right to be, but let's face the truth. Each of us has allowed resentment, anger, vengeance, pride, lust, and many other vices to creep into our hearts and minds and to some degree, take up residence in our lives. Maybe it's a little, maybe it's a lot. Furthermore, we too easily allow social media, pornography, and hateful rhetoric to influence us. For some, it corrupts us to the point that we feel justified for hurting, exploiting, and even destroying others. I know this to be true for me, and look where a life of selfishness and willfulness got me—a purgatory behind bars.

"Everyone in this room knows the will of God. *We know it* in our bones, but honestly, folks, do we give it our all, like the vigilant and faithful servant? I know I don't. We children of Adam cannot be condemned to hell merely for having defects of character or for our inevitable failure to do the will of God, but neither can we children of Eve expect quick admittance into heaven upon our death, no matter how vigilant we servants are. We are sinners!

"My brothers and sisters, whether I was serving time in Penbrook Correctional or walking free with you today, I am in purgatory! I need you to pray for me so that I will receive the grace of God to repent for the things I do each day that displease him. God help me, but I don't want to die only to discover too late that, in spite of my baptism, I have much to repent for.

"Never in a million years can I ever make up for the heartache and loss I caused the family and friends of those two innocent little girls I killed so long ago. All I can do, all I hope to do, is to spend the rest of my life in this purgatory outside the walls of Penbrook. Only with your constant love, your supportive prayer, and your encouraging fellowship can I live a life of amends, repentance, and discipleship to the best of my God-given abilities. As a third kind of servant, we must at least try to be a more vigilant and faithful servant of our lord and master. Referring to verse 47, I would justly deserve a *severe beating* for my sins when I die and prefer it over being consigned to spending eternity with the purely wicked. A beating I can take for not doing all I could or should to lead others to Christ our savior, but not hell. Nope, not going there!

"We must also be mindful and considerate of those living among us, as well as those living within the walls of our nation's prisons and jails, who represent the fourth servant in the master's household (Luke 12:48). Here I am referring to men and women who do not have the mental, moral, or spiritual development to be aware of God's will or his saving grace, but they nevertheless often do bad things—sometimes terribly hurtful things. These folks deserve constant, but compassionate supervision and care for the sake of their safety and our own. Under no circumstances should a man who is developmentally impaired or suffering from debilitating mental illness be put in solitary confinement, tortured, or worse, executed! May these poor folks of the master's household suffer less in purgatory than me.

"Thank you all for the honor you have given me by listening to my story. Remember Luke 12:42–49. In closing, I ask that everyone please stand, close your eyes, and join me in opening your heart, mind, and soul to a favorite prayer of mine: *O my Jesus, forgive us our sins, save us from the fires of hell, and lead all souls to heaven, especially those most in need of thy mercy.* Let the world hear us say *amen*!

"Now, how about we call Fr. John to come to the microphone and lead us in a blessing of our dinner? While we wait for Fr. John to make his way to the microphone, I want to announce the St. Jude parish jail ministry is meeting here next Tuesday night at 7:00 p.m. Anyone interested in learning more or lending a hand in this important ministry is surely welcome. All right, here's Fr. John."

Epilogue

―⚉―

Ten years later

It's a cool and dry morning in mid-spring 2036 when I pull up to the North Bedford Elder Care Center. It took a day and a half to drive here, but I didn't need a fancy global assist device or whatever these gadgets are called these days. Street maps do me just fine, thank you. My old friend Tommy Boy, from cellblock B, is already waiting for me under the front awning, so we throw his bag in the trunk and head off for our fifteen-hour journey in search of answers.

Two hotel stays, six meals, and at least a dozen rest stops later, we arrive at our final destination three states away. The state board of prisons is located inside an imposing granite office building, but we manage to find a parking spot at the public library two blocks away. Tommy Boy and I, both using canes in our right hands, slowly walk the distance along sidewalks buckled by tree roots.

It takes some time, but we eventually climb the twenty-seven steps to reach the huge marble and gilded lobby. A directory says the office of the state board of prisons is on the second floor, so thankfully, there's a bank of elevators waiting to give us a lift. We reach the frosted glass door of room 211, where we immediately recognize the logo—the same one we had on our old coveralls at Penbrook. The logo consists of two hands clasped in a handshake. The hands are handcuffed together, but the chain connecting the two cuffs is broken. I still think that logo is pretty cool. Tommy Boy thinks we should knock first before entering. Well, I understand. His knees and mine are shaking; prison etiquette is deeply ingrained. But fortune favors the bold, they say, so I open the door and walk right in.

There's a heavy oak counter running the length of the front office, with a two-foot-wide hinged countertop that lifts aside to allow people to enter or exit. We wait patiently for someone to assist us. After a minute, a woman seated at a desk facing us looks up, smiles, and asks how she can help us. Before I have a chance to speak, Tommy blurts out, "We want to know what happened to 34286. Is he dead? Did they kill him?" Tommy Boy is a trifle keyed up.

The woman, who looks to be in her late fifties, stands up, straightens her dress, and approaches the counter. She has a warm, disarming smile and asks us our names and who 34286 might be. After our hearts calm down and we start breathing easier, we introduce ourselves.

She jots down our names, prison numbers, and dates and place of incarceration on a piece of paper. Her pencil stops in midair, however, at the name of *Penbrook Correctional*. Looking up at us, she says Penbrook closed down completely about fifteen years earlier. The state still owns the land, she says, but the prison was torn down. Apparently, Walmart built a superstore on the site, but terminated its lease after a few years back.

"Who would have guessed," she says smiling, "that a huge, abandoned box store would be transformed into a model full-service regional branch of the immigration and naturalization service? Well, anyway, you said that prisoner 34286 was incarcerated in cellblock C of Penbrook in the summer of 2023, is that correct?"

"Yes, as best we can recall."

She smiles again and says to please have a seat while she does some checking.

Five minutes later, we see her through a large glass window into the back office showing several files to an older man, probably her supervisor. The man studies two files placed before him and consults the information we supplied to the woman. What are they talking about? Then the gentleman follows the woman back into the records room, while we wait another five minutes. The supervisor, followed by the female clerk, comes out to the service desk and introduces himself, and respectfully asks us to produce some form of personal identification. Comparing this information to our case files, he returns our IDs to us and the files to his clerk. Removing his glasses and absentmindedly polishing them with a tissue, he looks up and says that prisoner 34286-10 is not referenced in our files or those of warden Allen Cartwright, now deceased. Furthermore, a cross-check by inmate number shows that there is no record for a prisoner 34286-10. In fact, he says, no prisoner with that number had ever been incarcerated anywhere in this state.

Tommy Boy and I can't believe what we're hearing. After being assured that there has been no clerical mistake or purging of prison records, we sit down and take a few minutes to wrap our minds around this mystery. Still in shock, we leave the office and make our way down the elevator and out the front door.

My old buddy and I are lost in our own thoughts, walking in the direction of our car, when we're forced to stop at a traffic signal. Just then, the bells of a nearby Catholic church, St. Monica, begin to toll. It's the noonday reminder for all people of good will to pray. Tommy Boy and I know that we both need to sit in that church; it's calling loud and clear for us come inside.

Living in the late fourth century, St. Monica prayed her whole life for her wayward son, Augustine, to turn away from his life of selfish pursuits and turn his life over to Jesus. Thank God for her prayers! Her gentle statue greets us as we enter the sanctuary.

Picking a seat in a back pew, I sit with my head between my hands, trying to understand the crazy story of my own life, along with this latest information. That's when, in prayer, Jesus shines a light on 34286-10, who is alive in my heart. It's almost as if I can see him right here, right now, walking outside the cells at Penbrook. He is every man and every woman throughout history who sacrificed their lives so that others may be free and find eternal life. A guy's gotta believe what a guy's gotta believe.

The end

About the Author

Joe began his writing career in the fall of 1978, sitting under the branches of an oak tree beside Eagle Lake in the hills of Northeastern Kentucky. What started out as simply pouring his heart out to God in a spiral-bound notebook has evolved over the years into a powerful, prayerful exercise in which God speaks words of love, compassion, and healing to him—and to his readers. Joe finds himself in a deeper relationship with Jesus through his personal writing. With his writing, he hopes to bring others into deeper relationship with Jesus. He likes to say that he's just an ordinary Joe that has inspiring and thought-provoking stories to tell while he walks with his readers, if only for a few miles.

    Joe, a retired librarian, now lives with his wife in south central Michigan. When he is not at church or taking his dog, Lucy, for long walks, he can be found writing on a computer instead of a spiral-bound notebook. He is a member of the Catholic Writers Guild.

Printed in the USA
CPSIA information can be obtained
at www.ICGtesting.com
LVHW041737161124
796817LV00001B/132